D1165313

Babette Cole

JONATHAN CAPE
London

The Silly Book
The Slimy Book
The Smelly Book
The Hairy Book

This edition first published in the United Kingdom in 2001
by Jonathan Cape, The Random House Group Limited,
20 Vauxhall Bridge Road, London SW1V 2SA

1 3 5 7 9 10 8 6 4 2

All four titles first published by Jonathan Cape

The Random House Group Limited Reg. No. 954009

A CIP catalogue record for this book is available from the British Library

ISBN 0 224 04767 1

Printed in Hong Kong by Midas Printing Limited

THE Silly BOOK

If you look closely you'll agree,
there are some silly sights to see.

CUPIG
BOOPER SCOOPER

Silly people passing by
have silly walks
that you can try!

Silly ears

and silly necks,

silly noses,

silly specs.

Silly beards

and silly teeth,

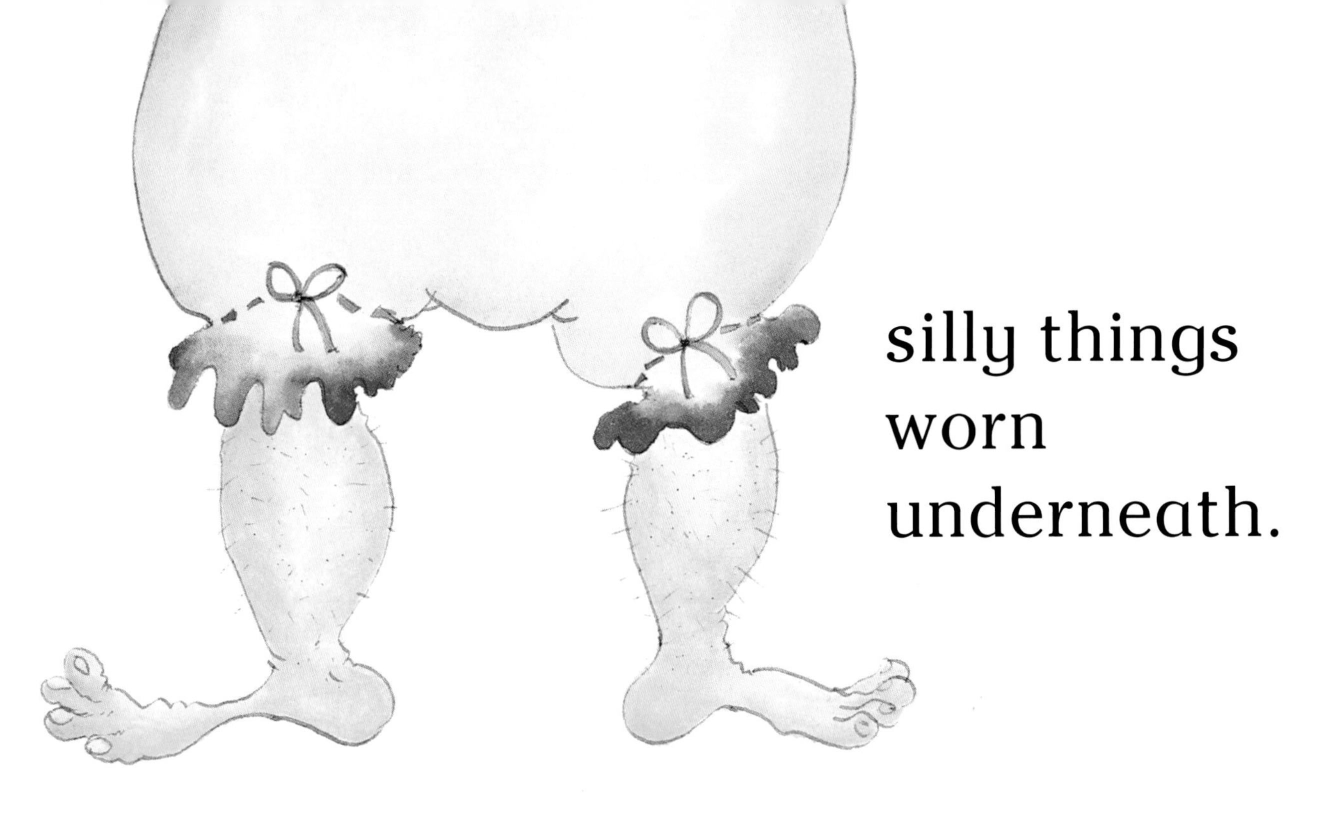

silly things
worn
underneath.

Silly hats are there to hide
some very silly heads inside!

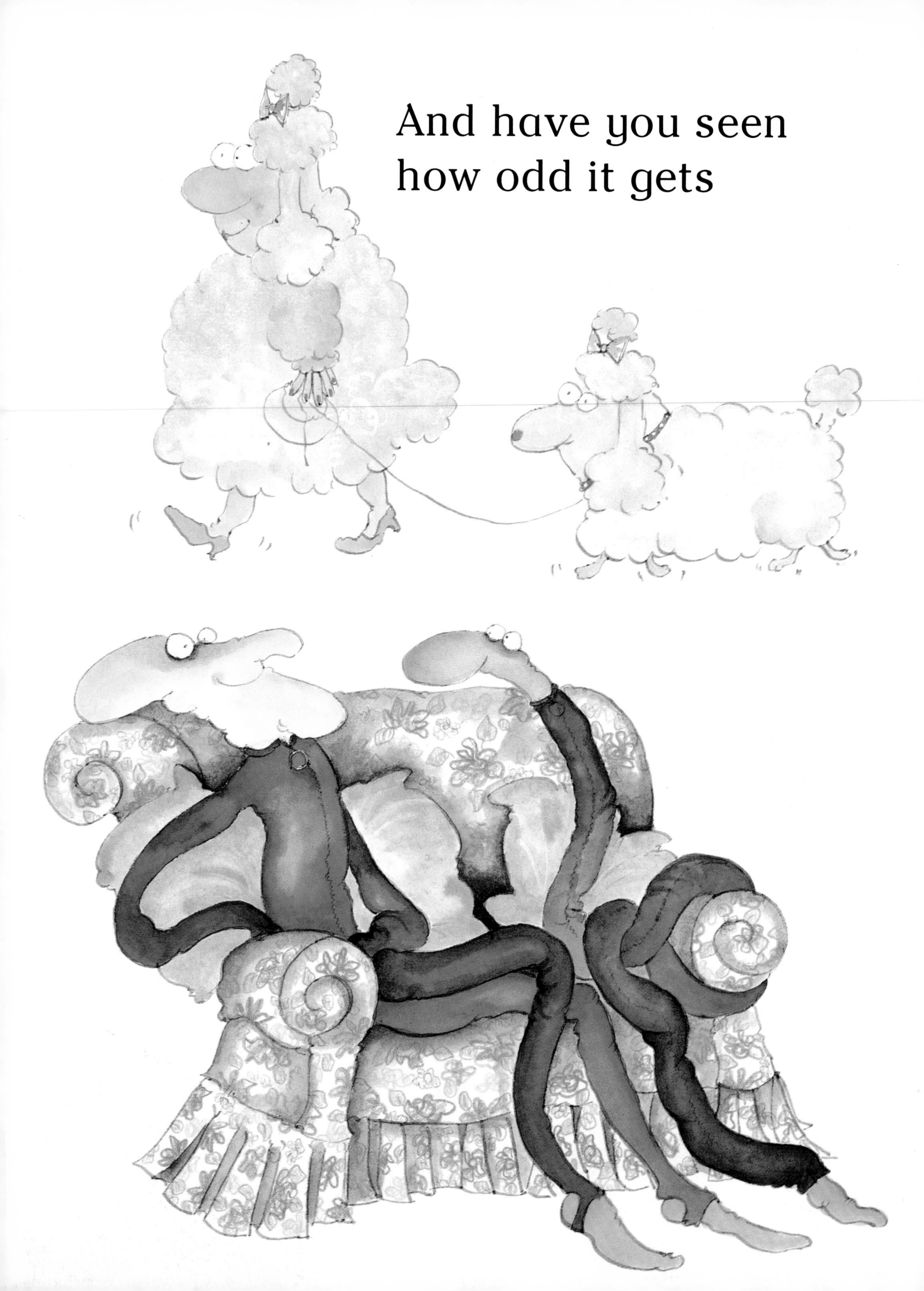

And have you seen
how odd it gets

when silly folks
look like their pets?

Silly zebras,

silly bears,

silly sharks

and silly hares.

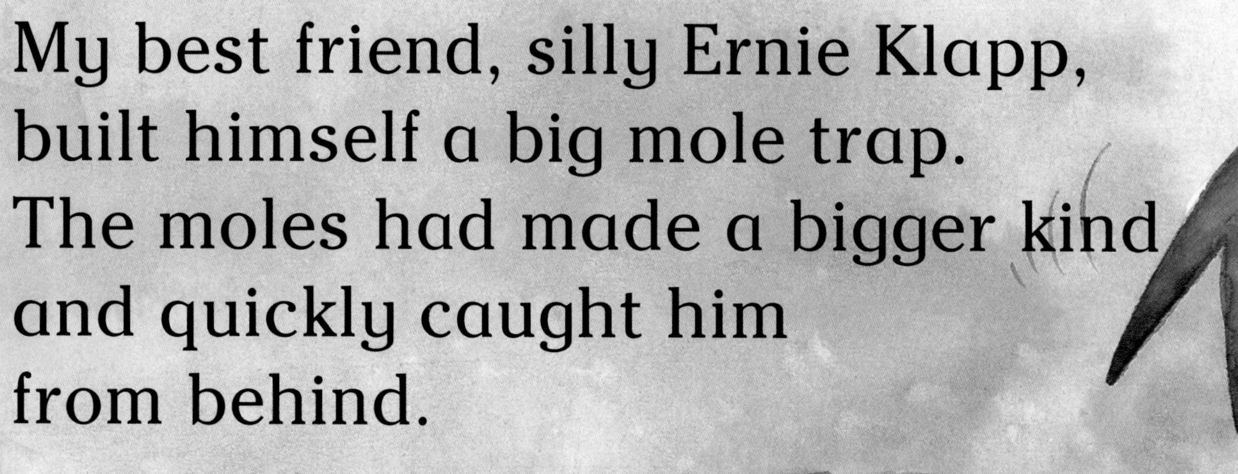

My best friend, silly Ernie Klapp,
built himself a big mole trap.
The moles had made a bigger kind
and quickly caught him
from behind.

B. O. Y. 2.

Some silly people like to fly,

I've never known
the reason why.

Babies eat some silly things,
like flies with wriggly legs and wings.

But grown-ups eat them just as well,
like wriggly frogs

and snails that smell.

My uncle Billy ate some fire.

His temperature went
higher and higher!

But auntie got the
teapot spout
and put poor
silly Billy out!

His friend, the Nabob of Namphilly,
had forty wives and all were silly.

They tickled him and not one stopped
until the poor old Nabob popped!

Don't play

silly party tricks

and scare
your friends
out of their wits . . .

With silly masks

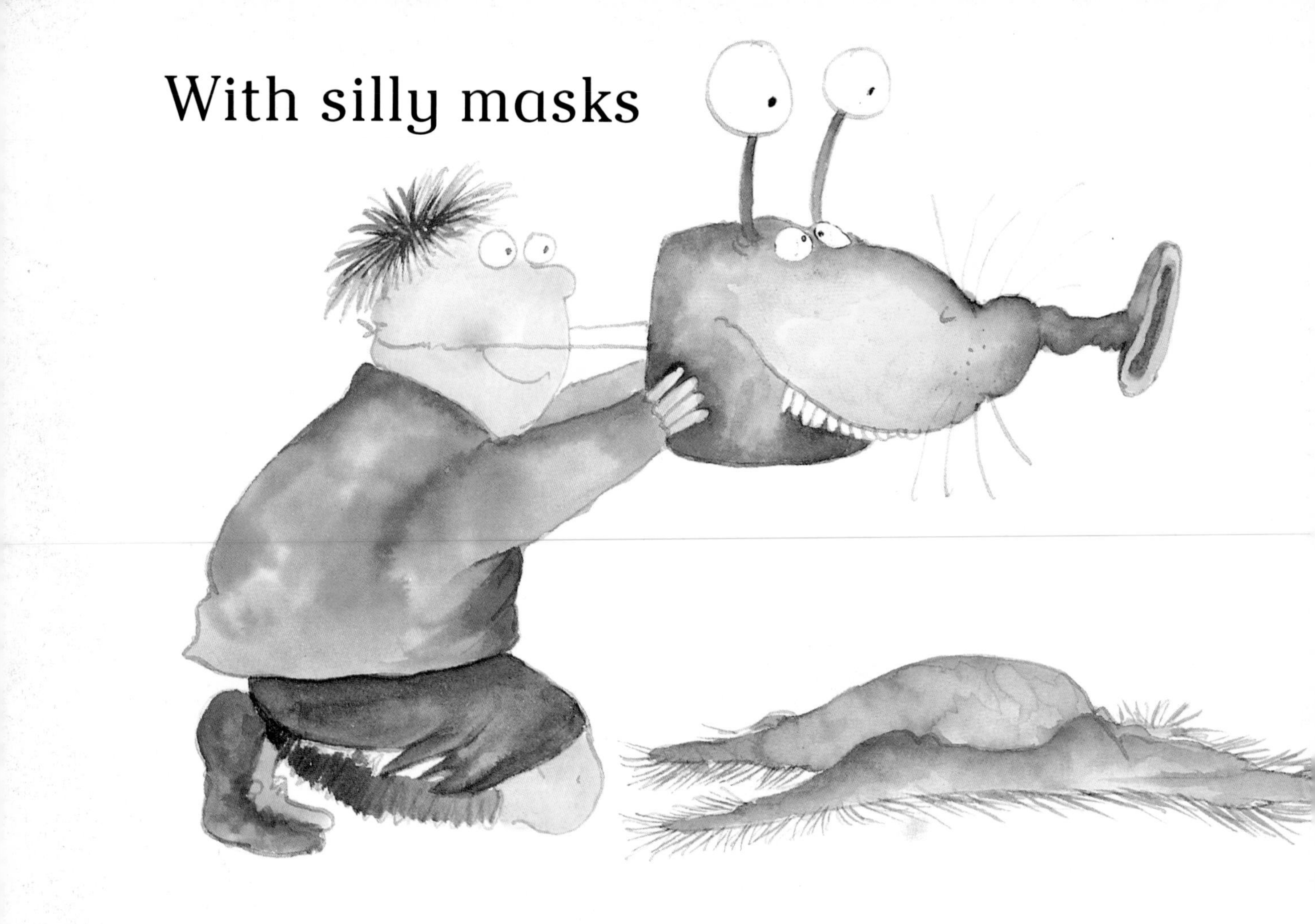

and silly sheets,

for they can cause some silly SHRIEKS!

I hate being dressed in silly best,

with collar and
cuffs all frilly.

I'd rather wear my
plain wool suit . . .

It doesn't look
as silly!

THE Slimy BOOK

Sticky, sludgy, slippy slime,

the sloppy, ploppy, creepy kind.

Slime in
my pocket,

in my shoe.

Is it
custard?

Is it glue?

Hello, slimy squids,

slugs,

snails,

and
slippery
toads
in slimy
pails.

Slimy worms on the lawn,

newts
from
ponds,

and green
frog-spawn.

Octopi with slimy limbs
eat little fish with slimy fins!

Fat ladies rub slime on their skin,

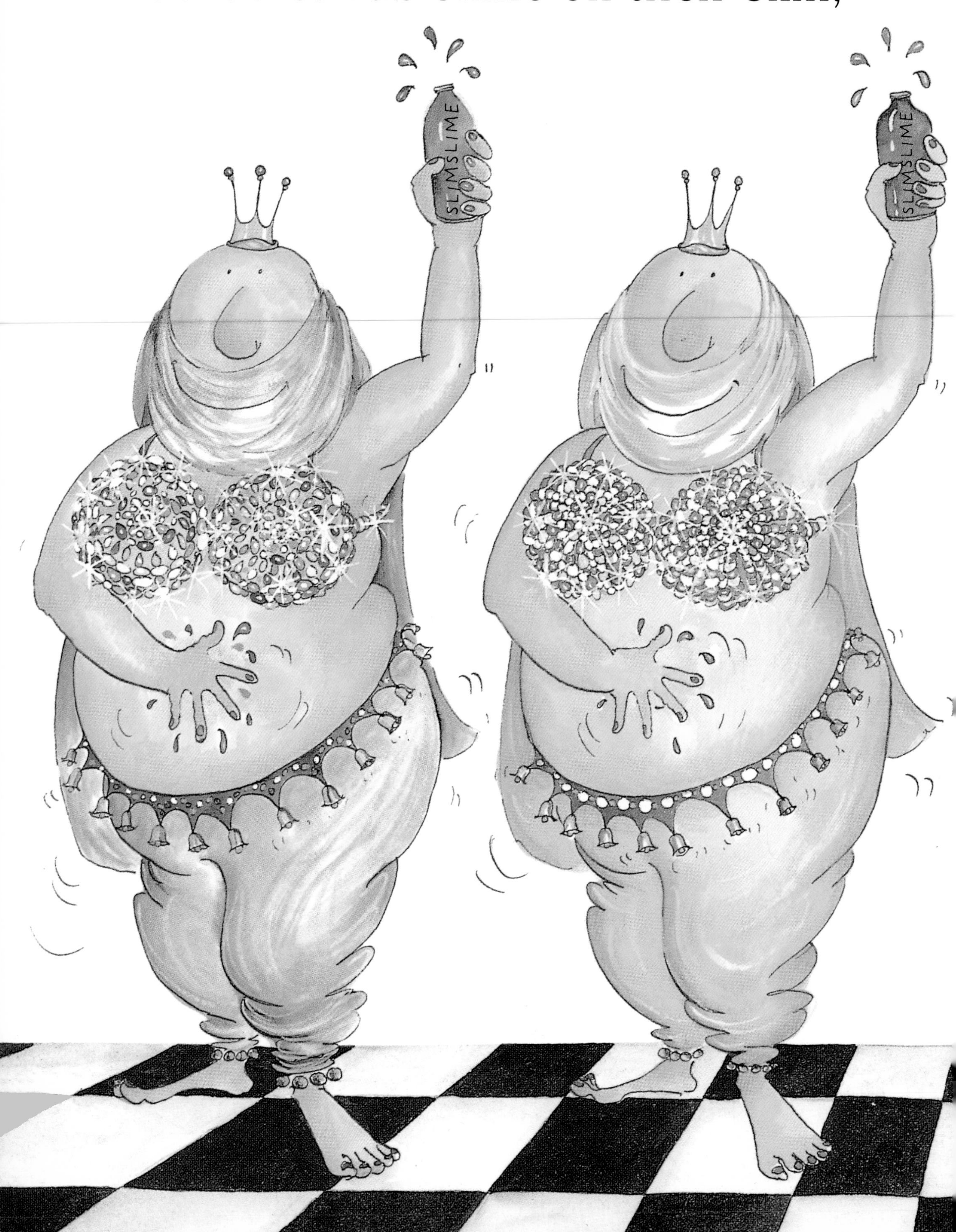

hoping it will make them thin!

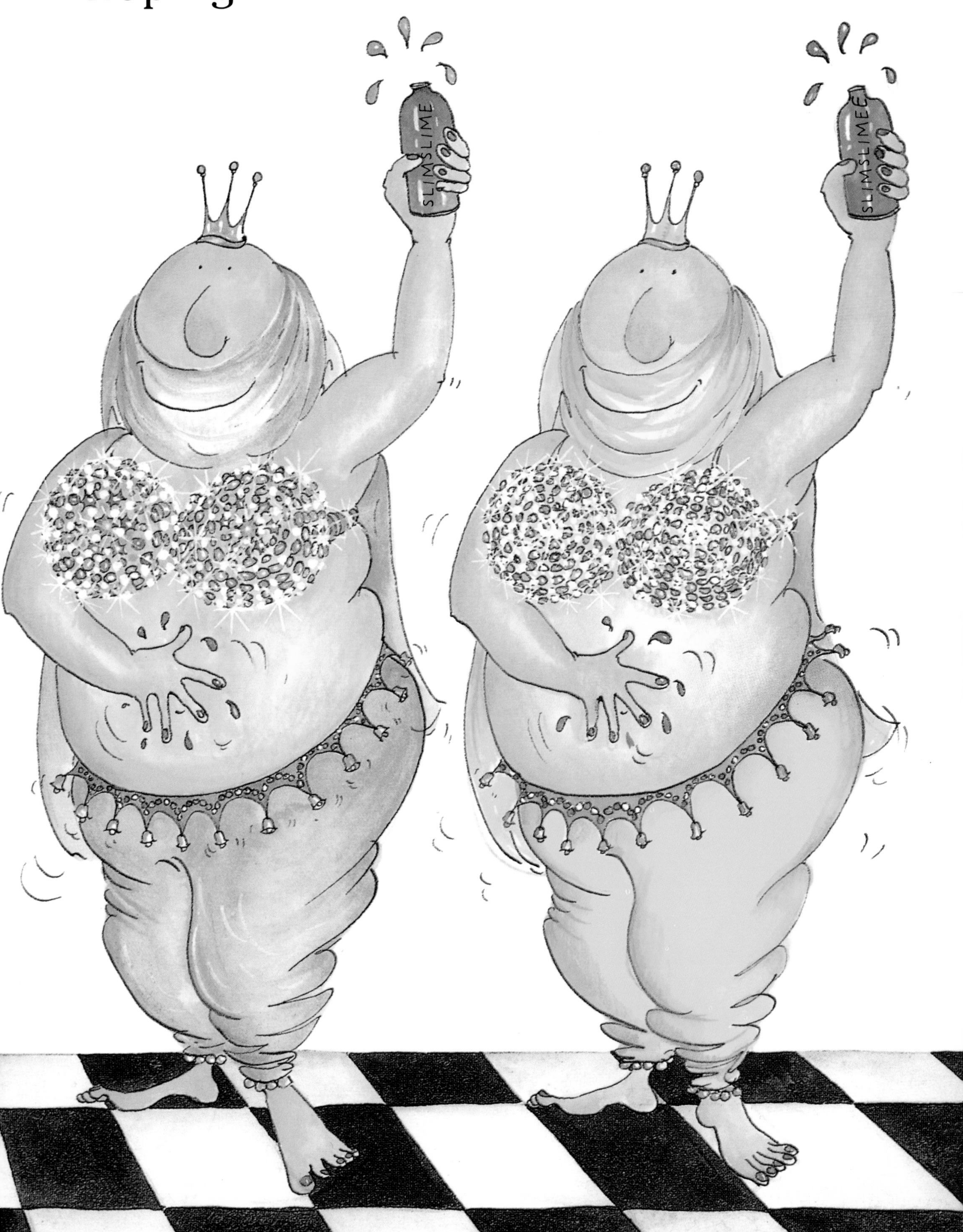

People with no teeth, it's said,
can't eat a slimy pickled egg!

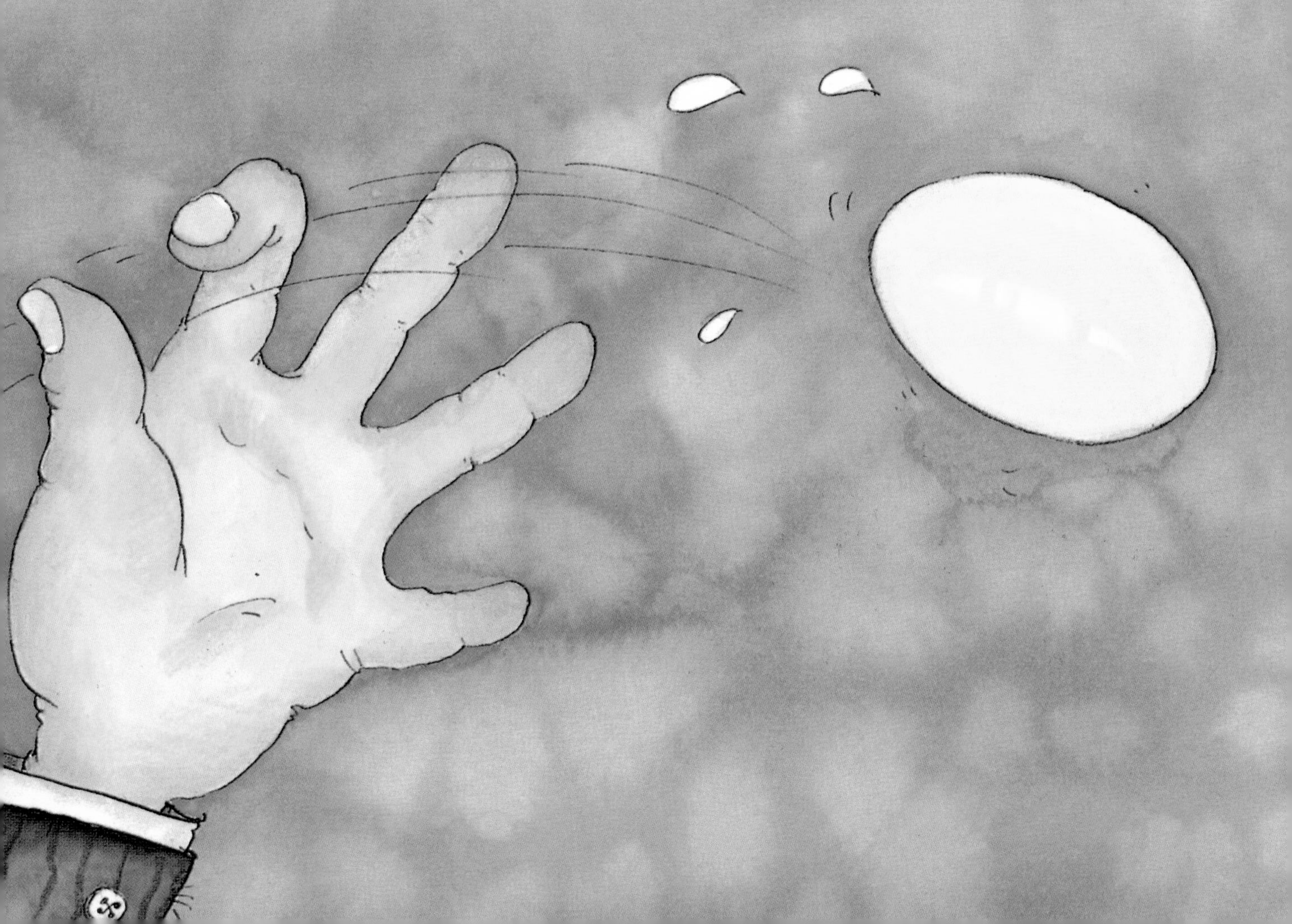

Slime loves dribbling down the drain,
and blocking all the pipes again!

Maybe it's
lurking
in the loo.
Careful! It could
pounce on you!

I wonder how it really feels,
slurping slimy
jellied eels . . .

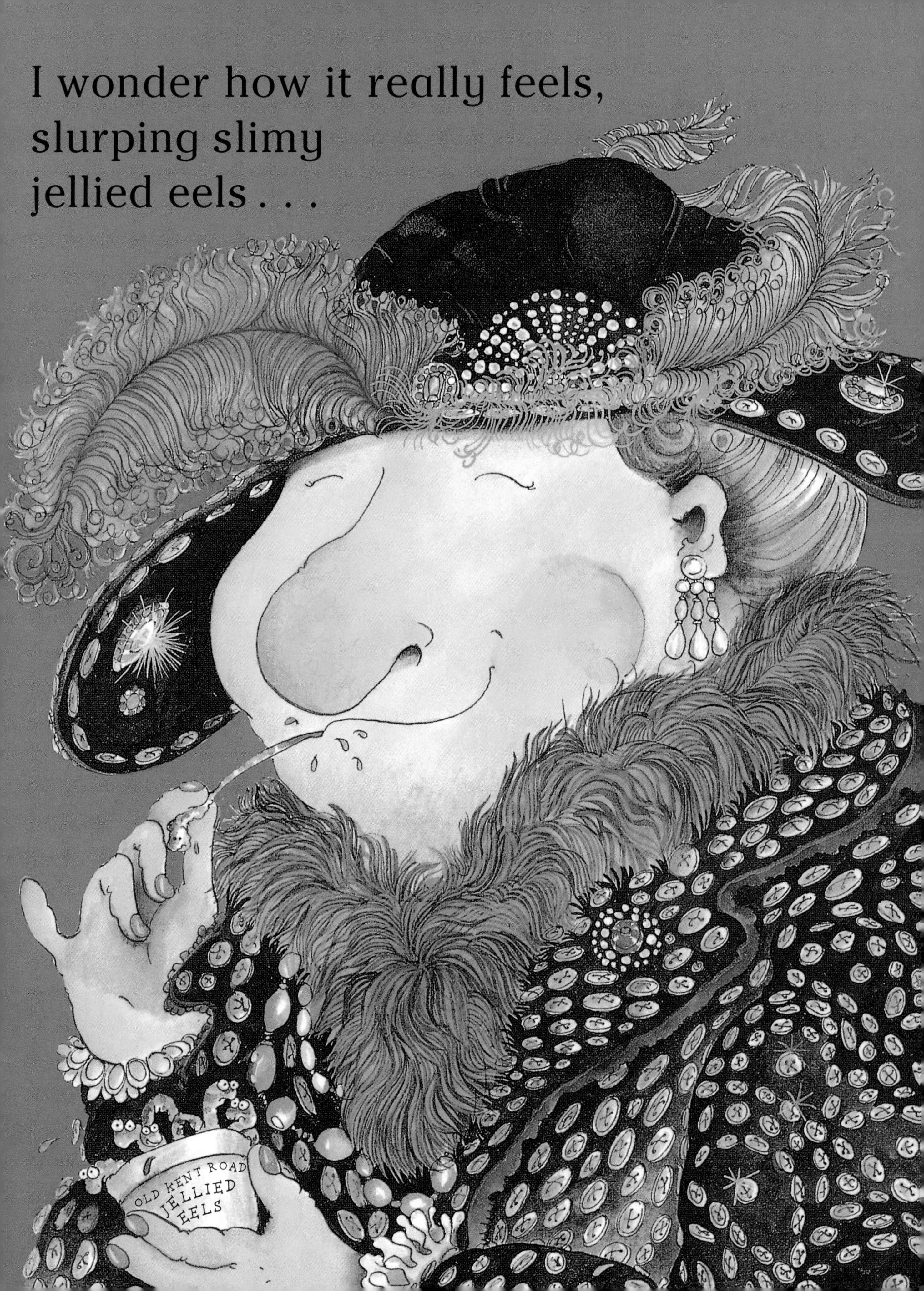

Here's someone having slime for tea,
I hope they never invite me!

TABLE
SLIME
Cup-a-Slime

Blimey! Slimy,
oodles noodles,
slimy sausages
for poodles . . .

Slimy butter,

slimy jelly,

slimy baked beans,

bulging belly!

I should have listened to my Mum,

who said, "Don't chew
that bubblegum!
It is the slimy
kind that clings . . .

to your nose and other things!"

And I wish
I hadn't tried
those horrid sweets
with slime inside!

With all the slime inside this book,
strange creatures came to have a look,

slimy green things straight from Mars,
and planets far beyond the stars,

they ate it up and left behind
trails of yellow
glistening slime!

Goodbye, you slimy things
I've seen . . .

I'm glad that you
were all a dream!

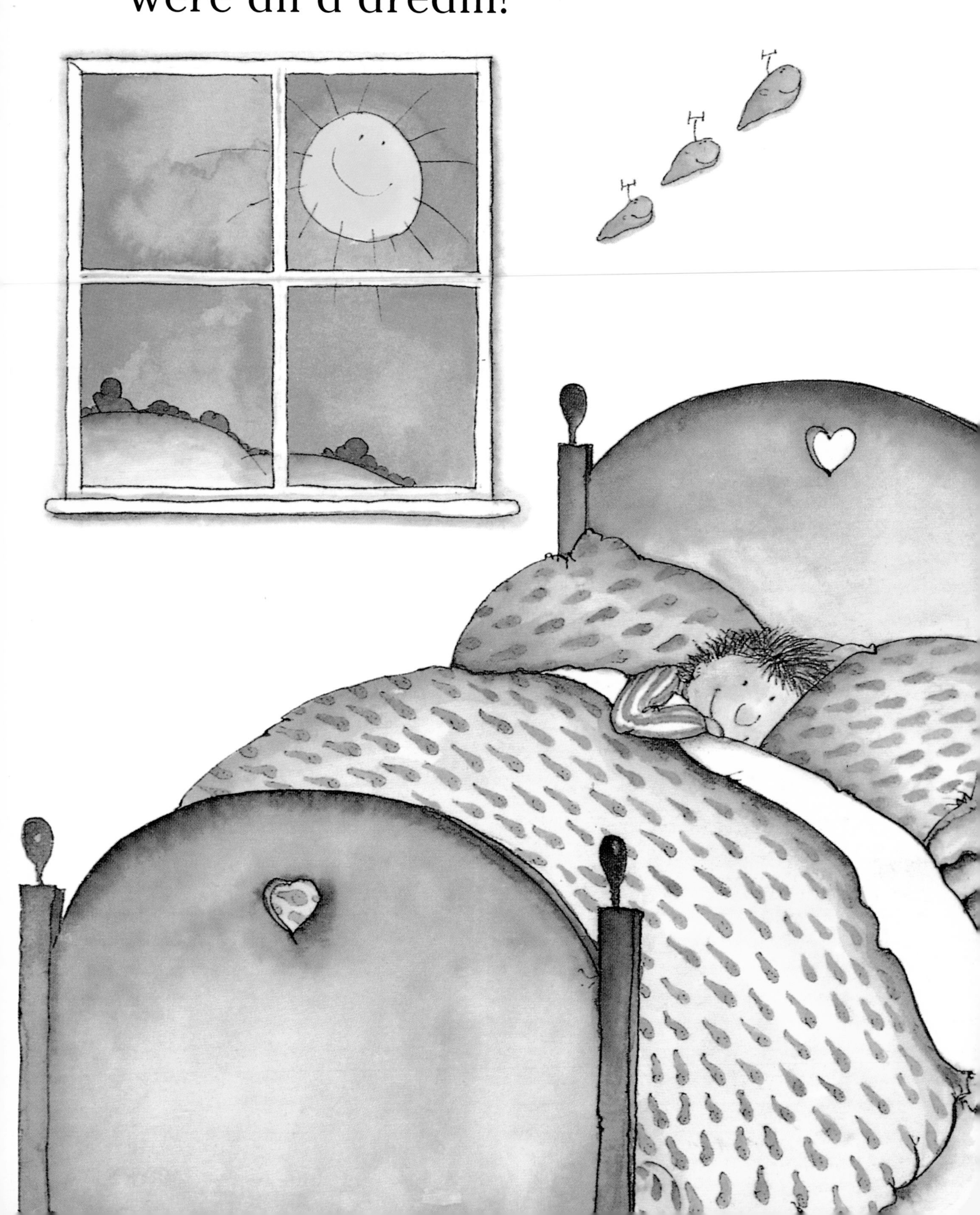

THE Smelly BOOK

Have you ever thought how many

things are really very smelly?

Smelly bags and
smelly bins

contain the most
revolting things.

Smelly cabbage,

smelly fishes,

smelly cheese

for smelly dishes.

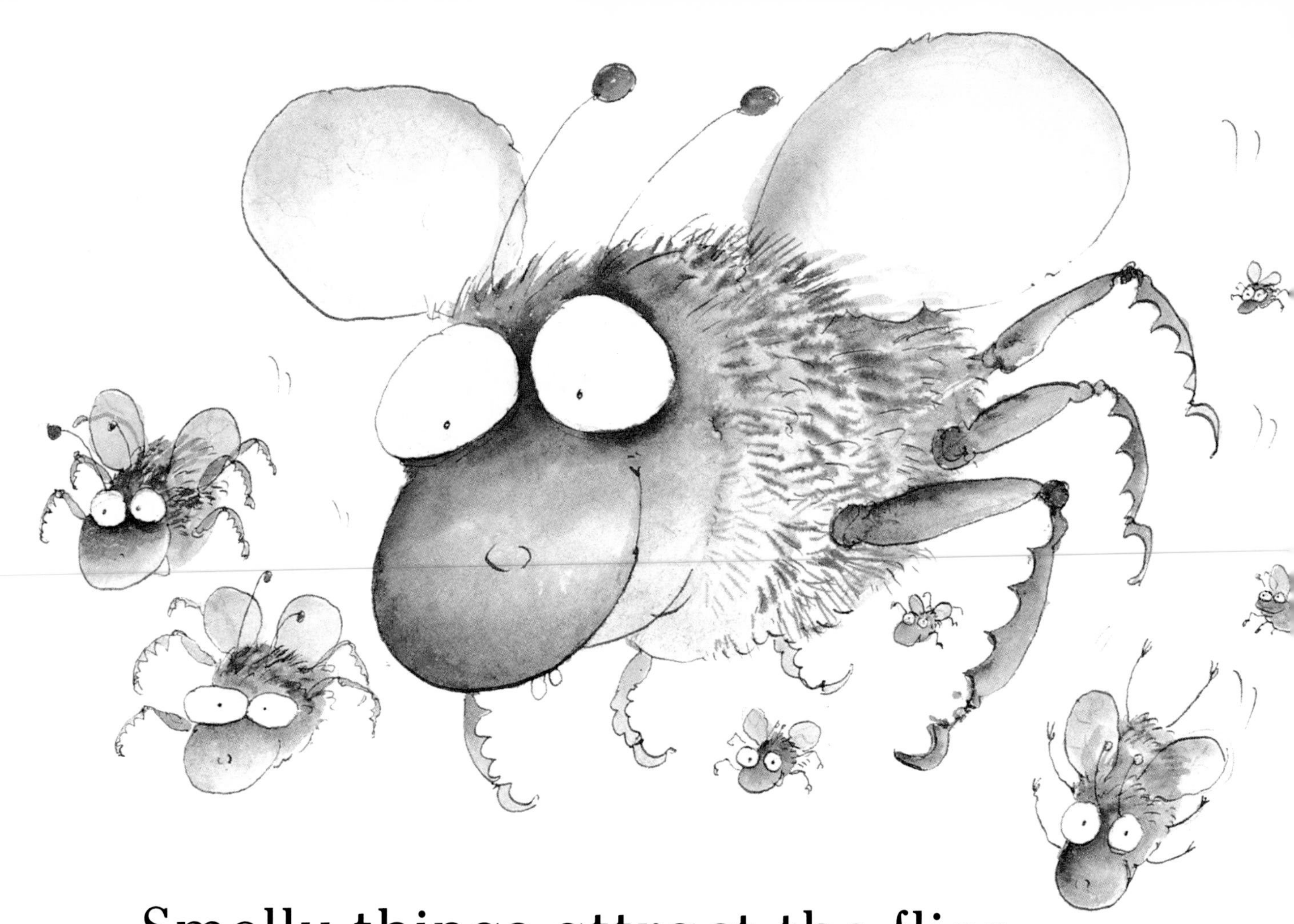

Smelly things attract the flies,
especially very old
pork pies.

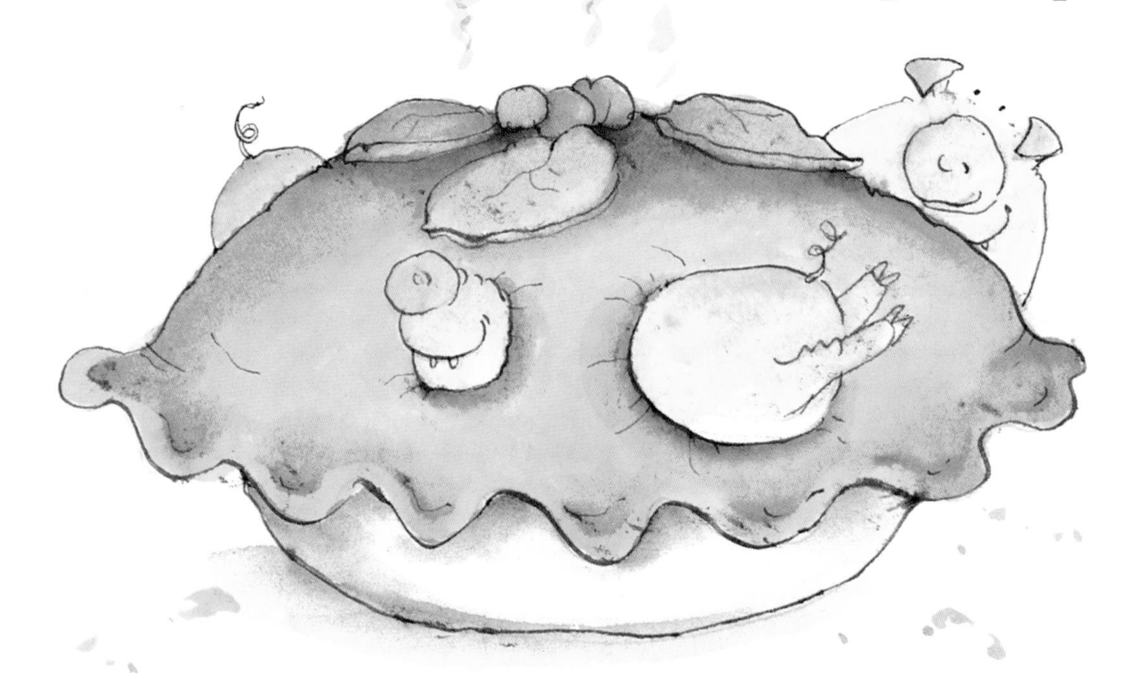

Camels have
a horrid pong,

warthogs can smell
very strong.

I think I would do a bunk

if I saw a smelly skunk!

Smelly pigs
and smelly mice

smelly ferrets are not nice!

Farmers are
a smelly bunch.
They can put you
off your lunch!

Stagnant puddles
smell so grim . . .

hold your nose
when you
jump in!

Smelly socks that
go quite stiff . . .

have the most
disgusting
whiff.

My dad's feet smell pretty bad,
sometimes it drives mum
quite mad!

Smelly bones make auntie swoon,

but smelling salts revive her soon!

Our dog likes to roll around

in smelly things left
on the ground.

But if I rolled around a drain

I'd never see my friends again!

Smelly babies
wail and bawl.

Smelly tramps don't
wash at all.

Smelly kids play smelly tricks

because some grown-ups are such twits!

Teacher said, "I smell a rat.
Who put this thing inside my hat?

. . . and who threw that rotten egg
at the science master's head?

Whoever did it was quite wrong

to blast the class with that stink bomb!"

He kept us in ’til after tea.

But never found out . . .

It was me!

THE

BOOK

Hair, hair, all kinds of hair,

Hair on your head . . .

and hair elsewhere,

Hair on legs,

hair in a wave . . .

Hair that you might have to shave.

Hairy hats and hairy feet . . .

Hair that doesn't smell too sweet!

Hair that's red,
Hair that's blue . . .

How many little hairs have you?
I know what will make you laugh . . .

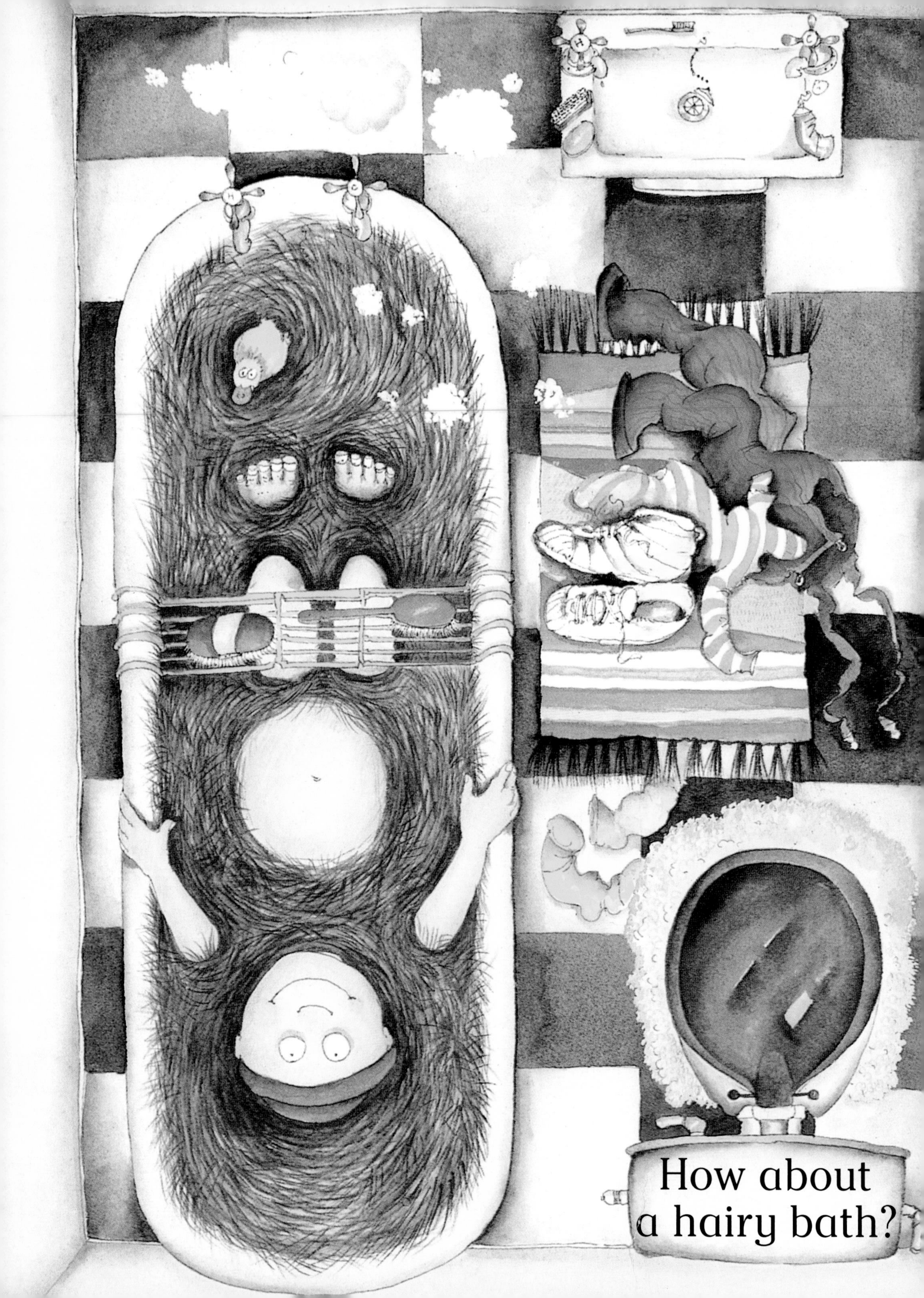
How about
a hairy bath?

Hairy coats
from hairy goats,

Hairy bogs with hairy frogs . . .

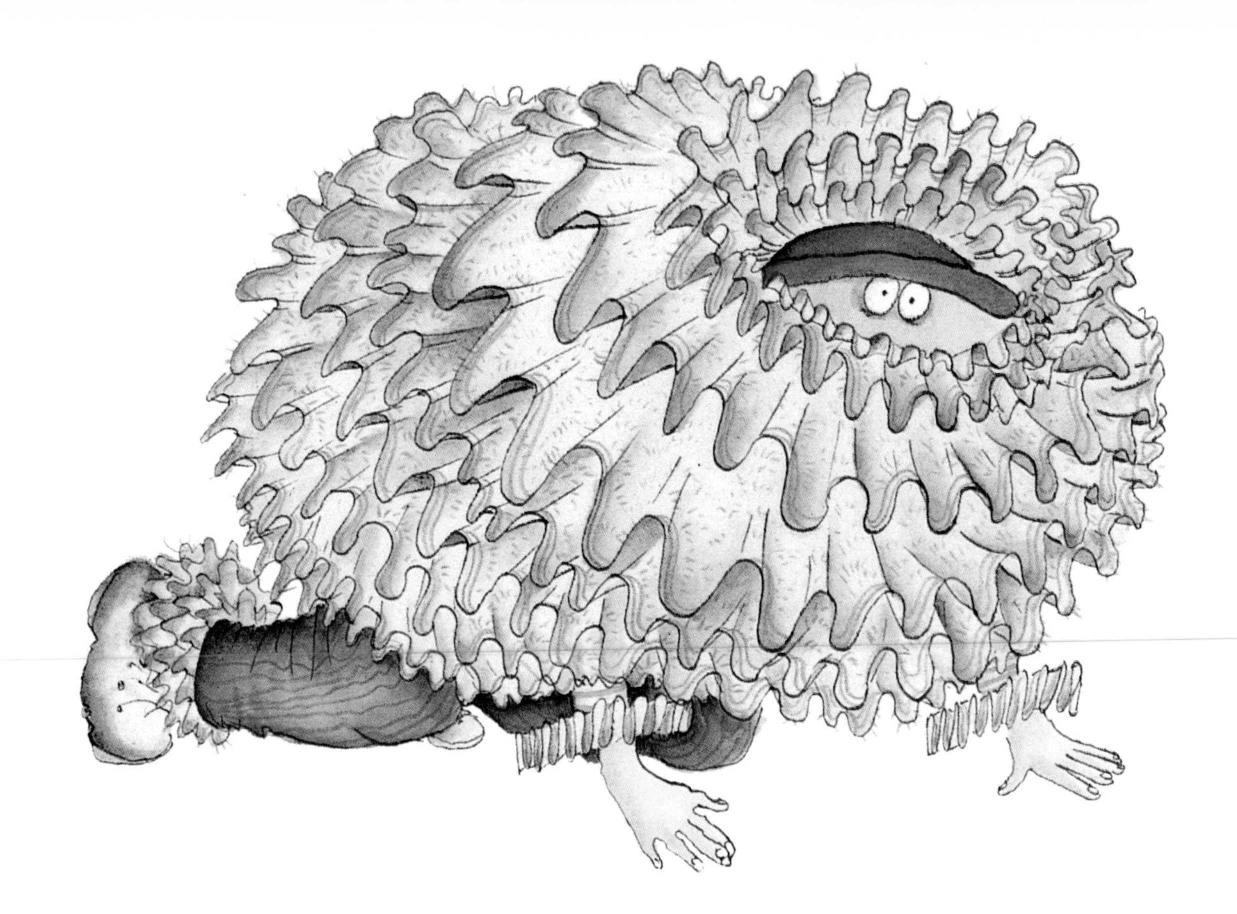

Hairy ruffs and hairy toughs,

Hairy cats and hairy rats
Have little fleas with hairy knees!

What hairy things, do you suppose,
Live up a big fat warty nose?

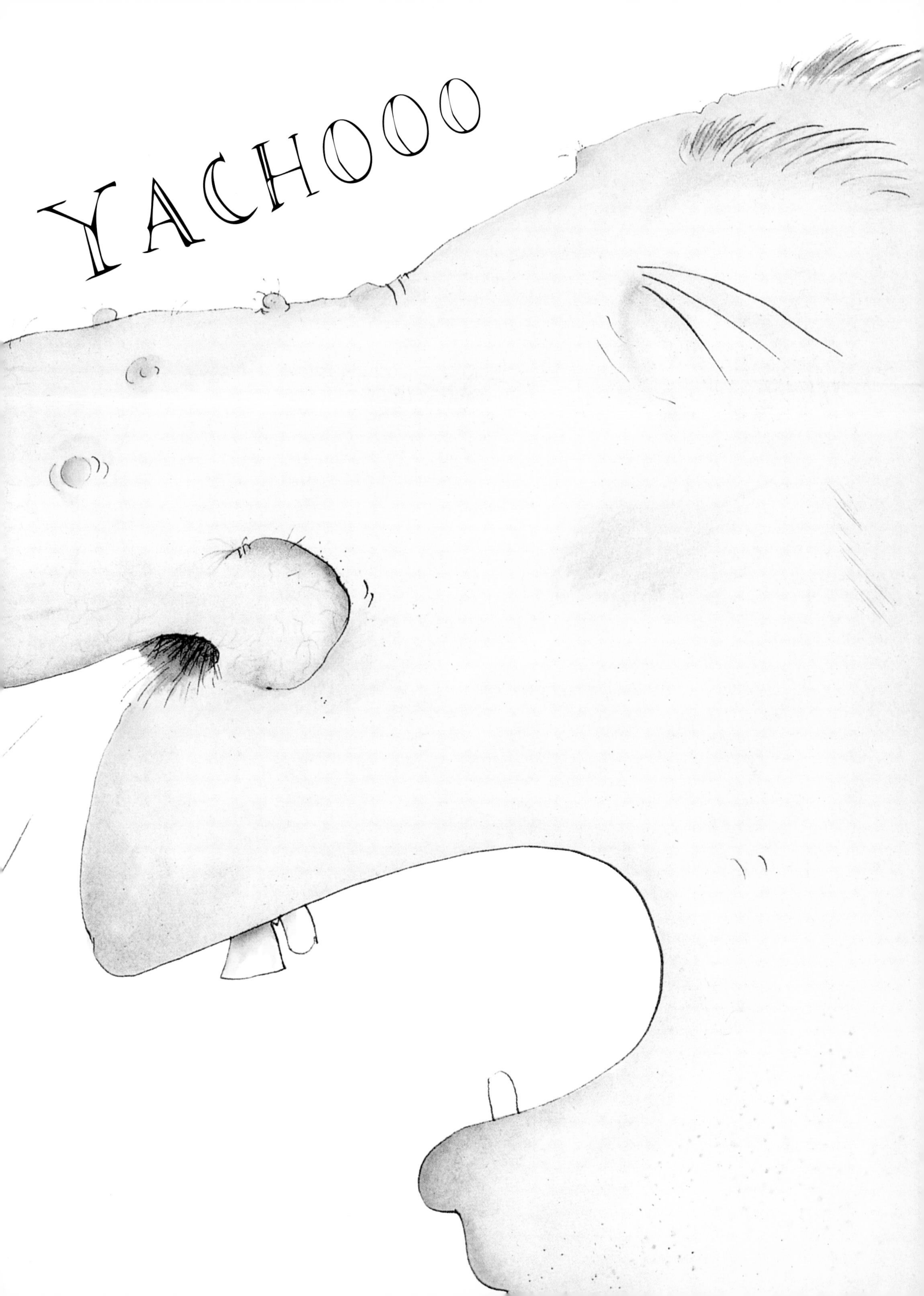
YACHOOO

Hairy pants

with hairy ants,

Hairy vests with hairy nests . . .

Have things that hatch

and make me scratch!

Hairy socks

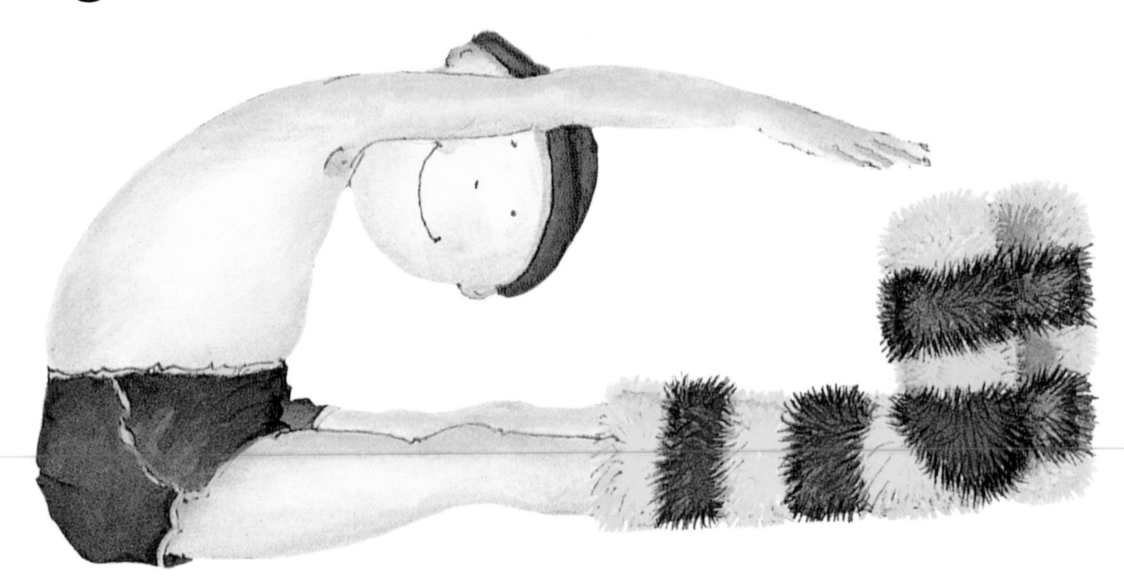

and hairy shirts,

and beefy
Scots with
hairy skirts.

Hairy nice

and hairy
scary . . .

Christmas tree with hairy fairy.

Hairy Mum and hairy Dad
Make me sneeze and wheeze like mad.

Grandad says, a pint of best
makes hair grow upon his chest!

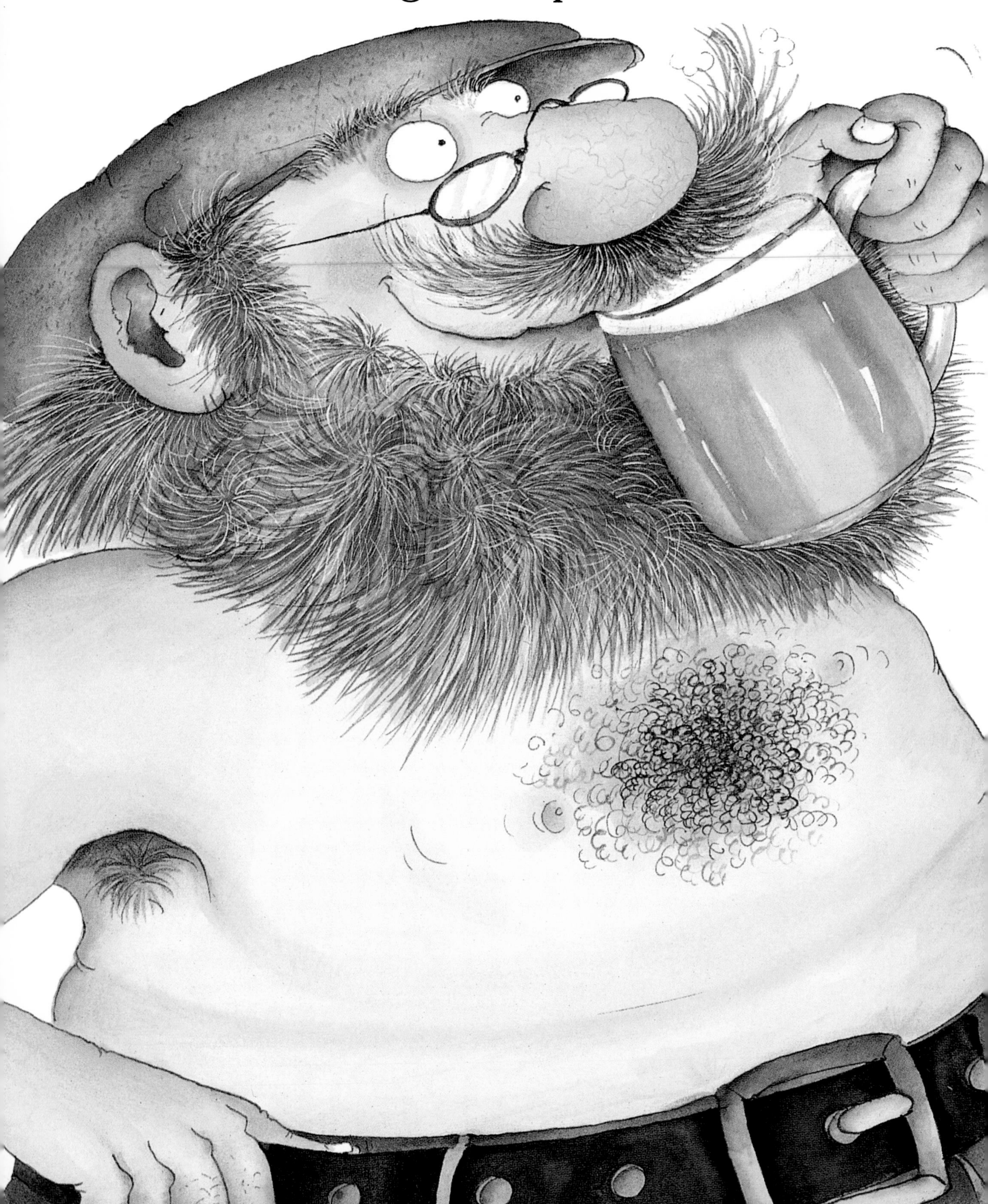

Hairy fruit and hairy bread . . .

Hairy things beneath the bed,

Hairy big . . .

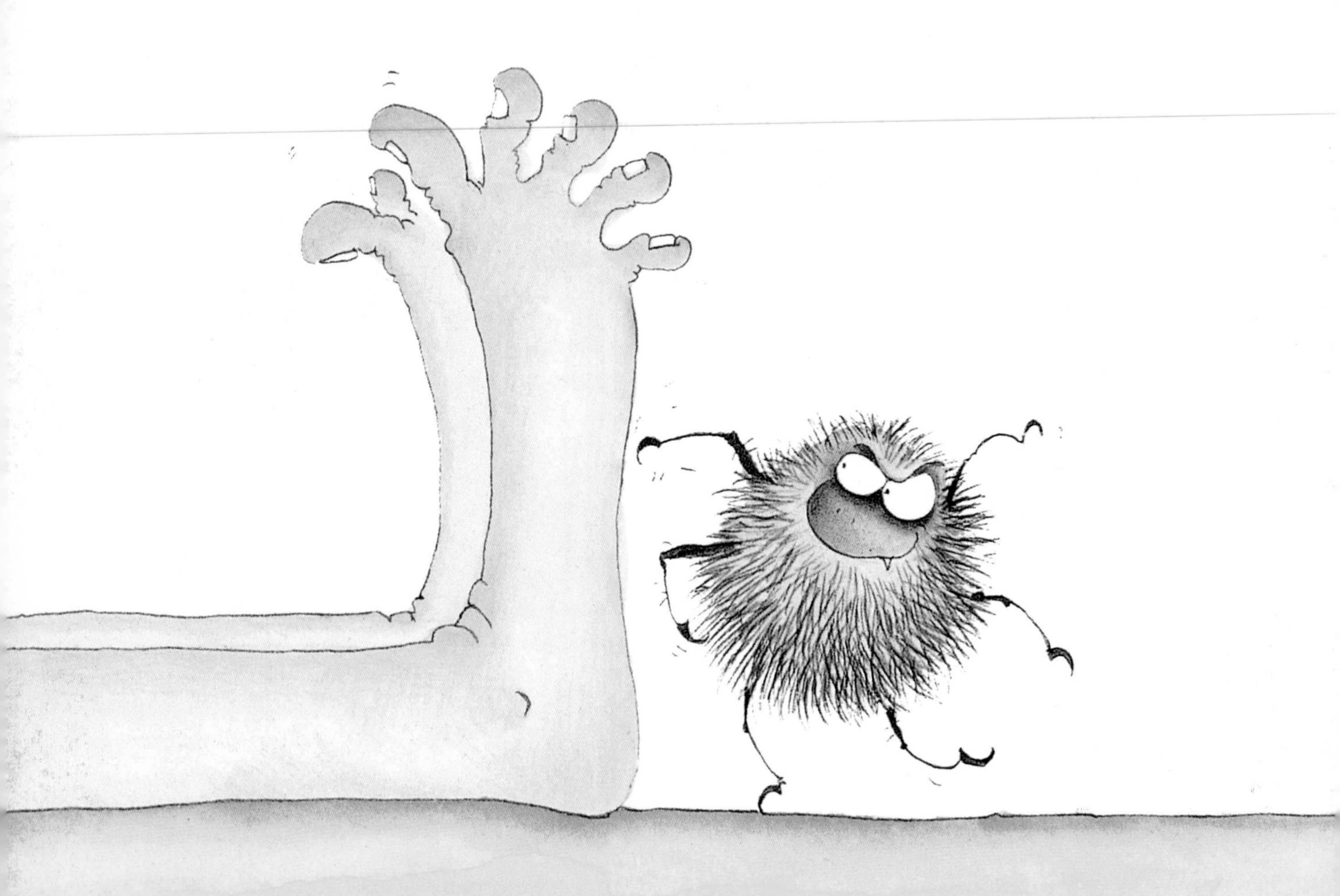

and hairy small,

I'm glad I have . . .

no hair at all!